D1505014

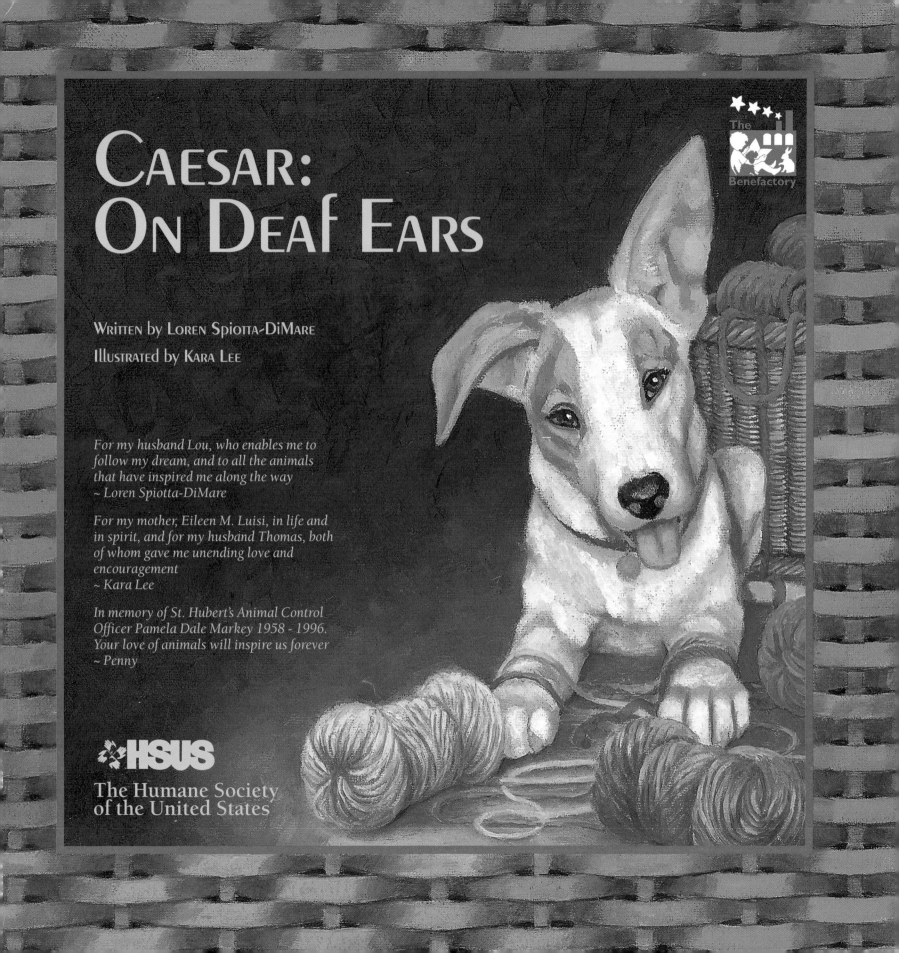

Caesar: On Deaf Ears

Written by Loren Spiotta-DiMare

Illustrated by Kara Lee

For my husband Lou, who enables me to follow my dream, and to all the animals that have inspired me along the way
~ Loren Spiotta-DiMare

For my mother, Eileen M. Luisi, in life and in spirit, and for my husband Thomas, both of whom gave me unending love and encouragement
~ Kara Lee

In memory of St. Hubert's Animal Control Officer Pamela Dale Markey 1958 - 1996. Your love of animals will inspire us forever
~ Penny

The Humane Society of the United States

Another train grumbled past the station. The two-week old puppies huddled close to their mother, shivering in the bitter wind. Rushing by, a woman nearly tripped over the family of strays. "Oh no," she cried. "You can't stay here!" She barely had time to call a shelter before boarding the train.

Soon an animal control officer drove up in his big, blue truck. He approached the strays slowly, trying not to frighten them. "It's OK," the man said gently. "I'll bring you back to St. Hubert's. We'll take good care of you there." The mother dog's tail slowly swept the ground. She seemed to know help had arrived.

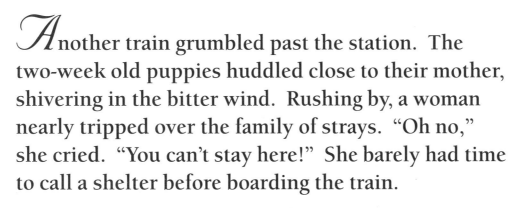

At first, the pups were sick and weak. "Give them plenty of good food and extra attention," said Penny, the shelter manager. The staff had to work hard to keep the pups alive. They placed the family in a separate, quiet room. A heat lamp hung over their padded box to keep them warm.

In just a few weeks, the puppies had doubled in size and were ready to be placed in homes of their own. They bounced around in their cage and pawed at the wire gate. Many visitors came to see the family. The woman who discovered them at the train station and called St. Hubert's ended up adopting the mother dog. Each day a puppy was adopted and left St. Hubert's with new owners.

One afternoon a young couple stopped by. The white pup wagged his little tail and licked the woman's hand. She ran her fingers over his soft, snowy fur. The pup nipped at her husband's shoe and undid his shoelace. "You're the one for us," the woman laughed. "I think with that Roman nose, we'll call you Caesar."

Caesar liked his new home. It was warm and safe. He had a soft bed, interesting toys and a big back yard to play in. There were so many wonderful things to chew on.

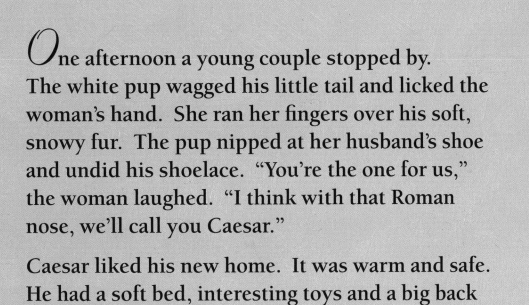

"No, shame!" his owner cried when she caught him chomping on a chair leg. Caesar didn't even turn his head. She scooped him up off the floor and plopped him onto her lap. But Caesar slipped right off and pounced on a pillow. "Drop it," the woman commanded sharply. But he kept tearing his prize with tiny puppy teeth. "Bad boy," the woman said, taking away the pillow, and giving him a chew toy. "I know your teeth hurt, but you just can't eat the furniture."

"Come, Caesar, I'm home," the man called a few days later, as he slammed the door behind him. But there was no sign of Caesar. Then the man stepped in a big puddle on the floor. "Oh no, not again!" he wailed. Hearing his voice, the woman ran into the room. "I took Caesar out every few hours," she explained. "He just doesn't seem to understand he must make puddles outdoors, not indoors!"

Her husband muttered and groaned as he cleaned up the mess. "I don't know how to train this dog," he sighed.

"All pups get into trouble," said his wife. Let's be patient. It takes time to learn house rules."

*B*ut weeks went by, and Caesar didn't learn at all. He never came when he was called. He wouldn't stop chewing or barking when they told him "No!" The pillows and rug all had ragged edges. A favorite shoe was in shreds.

Caesar's owners became desperate. They began locking him in the kitchen when they went out. But one afternoon he escaped. He leaped on the couch and ripped the cushions. He knocked over the potted plants and slid in the dirt. Then he grabbed the dining room curtains and started to play tug of war. His owners walked in the front door just as the curtain rod crashed to the floor.

"Oh no, Caesar! Look what you've done!" the woman cried out. "What are we going to do with you?" Munching happily on his curtain, Caesar didn't even look up.

"Is he just dumb?" her husband wondered.

"Maybe he's sick, " replied his wife as she reached for the curtains. "I better take him to the vet."

At the vet's office, Dr. Aaron said, "Let's have a look." He listened to Caesar's heartbeat and examined his eyes and ears. When the vet lifted Caesar's lips to check his teeth, the pup nipped at his fingers.

"Hold him in your hands with his back to me," Dr. Aaron requested. "Keep his attention focused on you." He took a few steps back and clapped his hands. Startled, the woman looked up. The pup didn't flinch. "Just as I suspected," Dr. Aaron said frowning. "Caesar can't hear."

"He's deaf?" asked the woman. "How can that be?"

"Well, he's mostly white and has such big ears — I think his father may have been a Bull Terrier. White Bull Terriers are sometimes deaf," answered the vet.

"Poor puppy," the woman thought as she left for home. "How will we ever be able to teach you anything?"

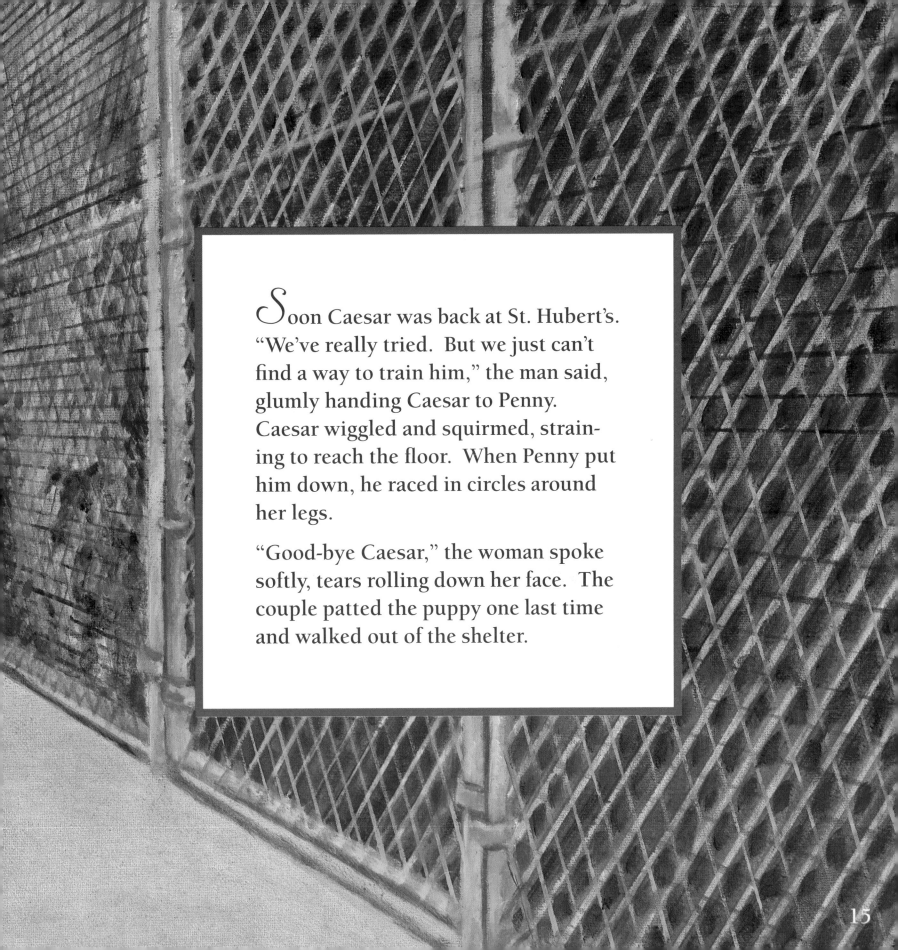

Soon Caesar was back at St. Hubert's. "We've really tried. But we just can't find a way to train him," the man said, glumly handing Caesar to Penny. Caesar wiggled and squirmed, straining to reach the floor. When Penny put him down, he raced in circles around her legs.

"Good-bye Caesar," the woman spoke softly, tears rolling down her face. The couple patted the puppy one last time and walked out of the shelter.

15

"We may have to put him to sleep," one of the shelter workers said.

Penny frowned. "Let's not give up on him yet. There must be a way to train him." Bending down next to Caesar she whispered, "I'll think of something. I promise, one day I'll place you with a family who will love and keep you forever." Caesar looked up into her eyes. But of course, he hadn't heard a word.

When Penny walked away, Caesar began to whine. He was lonely. But over the next few weeks, everyone at the shelter gave Caesar special attention. They took him for walks. They let him play in the office. He started to feel better. Penny watched him closely as he tried to follow each new friend.

"I'll teach you myself," she decided.

$\mathcal{P}$enny took Caesar home to live with her dog Bandit, and her two cats, Casey and Annie. This pup was not the first shelter orphan Penny brought to their house, so her pets were used to visitors. The dogs greeted each other with wagging tails and lots of sniffing. Then Caesar dashed off to chase the cats. As Bandit raced in between to protect his feline friends, Caesar skidded to a stop. "Good Bandit," Penny laughed. "You'll help me train Caesar, won't you?"

At dinnertime, Caesar finished first then poked his nose in Bandit's bowl. The older dog growled and snapped at him. The pushy pup jumped back. The next night, he'd forgotten, and reached for Bandit's food again. Bandit showed his teeth, and Caesar stepped away. "So you *can* learn quickly," grinned Penny as Caesar watched Bandit eat every bite.

Soon Caesar felt right at home. Even the cats would sometimes rub up against his soft, white fur. Like a shadow, Caesar followed Bandit everywhere. They chased each other all around the house. If Caesar ran too close to the stairs, Bandit pushed him away so he wouldn't fall. If he was rough with the cats, Bandit always came to their rescue.

*I*n the beginning, Penny often brought Caesar into the yard. Then when he'd made a puddle, she patted him, and led him back into the house. Bandit helped by setting a good example. Penny never yelled or spanked Caesar for accidents. Soon there were no more mistakes.

Still, every day was a challenge. It was hard to remember Caesar couldn't hear. At first Penny would pick him up and take him away when he misbehaved. Then she had a better idea! Catching Caesar chewing on a chair leg, she threw an old sock filled with beans near his hind legs. Caesar felt the "thump" as it hit the floor. He jumped and turned to look at her. She shook her finger at him. This became his signal for "bad dog."

She was careful to pat him every time he was a "good dog." Caesar tried hard to earn these loving rewards.

20

But Penny still needed a way to talk to Caesar, to keep him out of trouble. She soon stumbled on an answer. One night she cooked hot dogs for dinner. Caesar followed her from the sink to the counter - from the counter to the stove. His eyes never left her hand or those hot dogs! Penny popped a piece into his mouth. He stood on two legs, begging for more. "That's it," Penny thought. "I'll train you with hot dogs!"

Taking a tiny morsel of hot dog, Penny ran it across her hand and let Caesar lick her. She moved her hand up, then down, over and over with Caesar's eyes watching her every move.

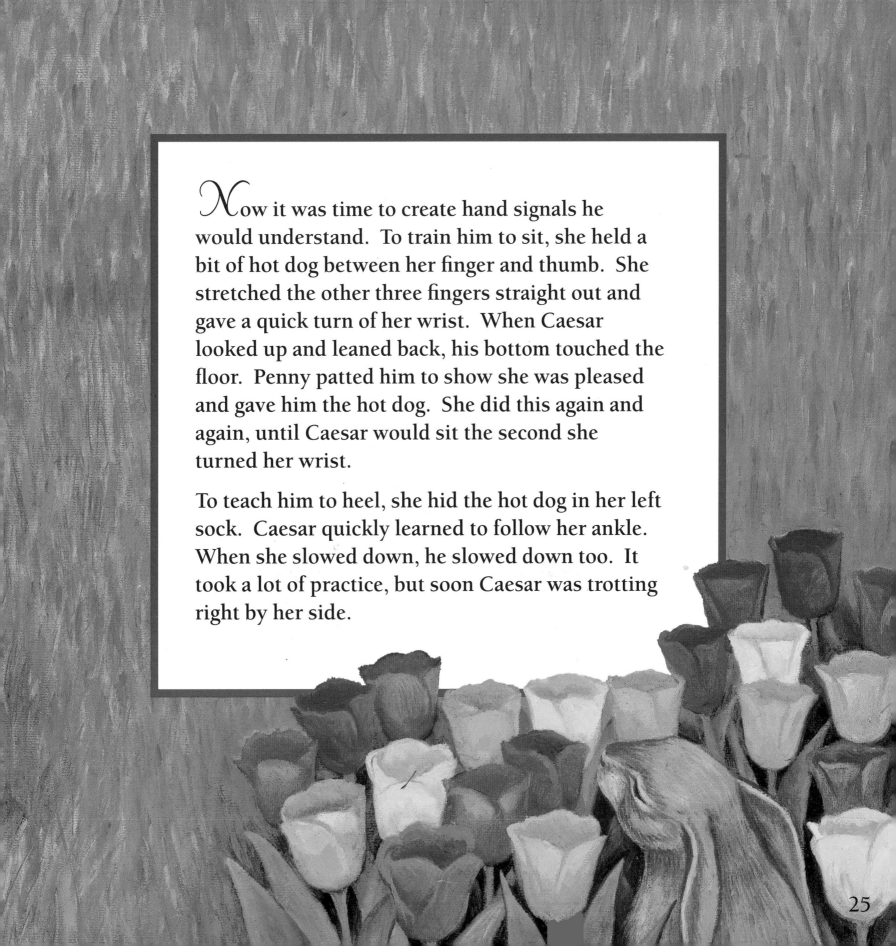

$\mathcal{N}$ow it was time to create hand signals he would understand. To train him to sit, she held a bit of hot dog between her finger and thumb. She stretched the other three fingers straight out and gave a quick turn of her wrist. When Caesar looked up and leaned back, his bottom touched the floor. Penny patted him to show she was pleased and gave him the hot dog. She did this again and again, until Caesar would sit the second she turned her wrist.

To teach him to heel, she hid the hot dog in her left sock. Caesar quickly learned to follow her ankle. When she slowed down, he slowed down too. It took a lot of practice, but soon Caesar was trotting right by her side.

25

Penny often brought Caesar along to St. Hubert's to be near her. Bandit came too. Most people train their dogs 15 minutes a day. But Penny trained Caesar for 10 to 15 minutes every hour for many weeks. Caesar was smart and learned quickly. Wherever Penny went, Caesar was close behind. Penny grew to love this special dog more and more.

"I don't think I'll be able to give you up," she said to him one night as Caesar rested his head in her lap. She scratched his neck and tickled his ears. When he turned to look at her, Penny touched her fingers to her face. This was his signal for "love me." Caesar happily kissed her cheek. Bandit nudged her hand with a cold nose. Penny laughed and hugged him too.

As the months went by, Caesar grew fond of the cats, though Bandit became his best friend. The two dogs were always together. They loved to race and chase each other.

One afternoon the mailman accidentally left the backyard gate open. The gate banged hard, and Caesar felt the "thump." Waking from his nap, he spotted a squirrel bolting across the street. Up he jumped, a white streak as he darted after the squirrel. Penny heard a honking horn and looked up. "No, Caesar," she shouted, terrified. But Caesar couldn't hear.

In a flash, Bandit dashed through the open door and out of the yard. He bumped Caesar hard on the hip, pushing him to the side of the road. The honking car wailed as it passed by.

Bandit and Caesar trotted back to Penny. She ran her hands over both, crying "Oh, Caesar - are you OK? Bandit - are you? Bandit, you're a hero!" She hugged both dogs at once, wiped away tears and smiled. "Well Caesar, Bandit says we can't spare you. I guess you're a permanent part of our family now."

andit and Caesar spend hours playing ball or chasing each other around their back yard. But when Penny calls them, Bandit circles Caesar and leads him into the house. "Good boy," Penny says to Bandit and pats him. Then she pats Caesar and waves in a backward motion—his signal for "good dog."

Glossary

Grumbled	made a low noise, growled
Huddled	crowded together
Strays	animals without homes or people
Bitter	harsh, stinging
Animal control officer	town worker who brings strays to a shelter
Adopting	take an animal home to keep
Roman nose	a long, curved nose
Chomping	chewing, biting
Patient	calm, waiting without complaining
Desperate	without hope
Vet	animal doctor
Bull Terrier	a strong, short-haired terrier
Glumly	sadly
Whine	a sad, begging sound
Orphan	without parents
Feline	part of the cat family
Misbehaved	did the wrong things
Signal	show with a message
Train	teach
Permanent	lasting, forever

The real Caesar

Special thanks to Penny, and to St. Hubert's Animal Welfare Center for providing research, photographs and other information regarding Caesar's story. St. Hubert's is a comprehensive community service organization dedicated to enriching the lives of animals and people. Founded in 1939, the nonprofit organization works to alleviate the neglect and suffering of companion animals, and to fostering humane attitudes. In addition to pet adoption and animal rescue, St. Hubert's offers other community outreach services including animal-assisted therapy, humane education, dog training classes and pet loss support therapy. For more information, call: (973) 377-2295.

The Humane Society of the United States, a nonprofit organization founded in 1954, and with a constituency of over 5.2 million persons, is dedicated to speaking for animals, who cannot speak for themselves. The HSUS is devoted to making the world safe for animals through legal, educational, legislative and investigative means. The HSUS believes that humans have a moral obligation to protect other species with which we share the Earth. Co-sponsorship of this book by The Humane Society of the United States does not imply any partnership, joint venture, or other direct affiliation between The HSUS and St. Hubert's. For information on The HSUS, call: (202) 452-1100.

Text Copyright ©1997
The Benefactory, Inc.
Illustrations Copyright ©1997
Kara Lee
Designed by Anita Soos Design, Inc.
Color Separations by Viking Color Separations Inc.

ISBN 1-882728-87-4
Printed in the U.S.A.
10 9 8 7 6 5 4 3 2 1

Published by The Benefactory, Inc.
One Post Road, Fairfield, CT 06430
The Benefactory produces books, tapes and toys that foster animal protection and environmental preservation.
Call: (203) 255-7744